P9-ARQ-779

Happiness
doesn't come from
Headstands

text and illustrations by
Tamara Levitt

Wisdom

Wisdom Publications
199 Elm Street
Somerville, MA 02144 USA
wisdompubs.org

Library of Congress Cataloging-in-Publication Data
Names: Levitt, Tamara, author.
Title: Happiness doesn't come from headstands / Tamara Levitt.
Other titles: Happiness does not come from headstands
Description: Somerville, MA : Wisdom Publications, [2017] | Summary: A story
about the search for happiness, and one girl's discovery that even in the
face of failure, peace can be found.
Identifiers: LCCN 2016015702| ISBN 9781614293897 (hardcover : acid-free
paper) | ISBN 1614293899 (hardcover : acid-free paper) | ISBN
9781614294054 (ebook)
Subjects: | CYAC: Happiness—Fiction. | Self-esteem—Fiction. |
Contentment—Fiction.
Classification: LCC PZ7.1.L4875 Hap 2017 | DDC [E—dc23
LC record available at https://lccn.loc.gov/2016015702

ISBN 978-1-61429-405-4   ebook ISBN 978-1-61429-389-7

21 20 19 18 17
5 4 3 2 1

Watercolor and Digital Painting by José Gascón.
Designed by Tamara Levitt. Set in Just the Way You Are.

Wisdom Publications' books are printed on acid-free paper and meet the
guidelines for permanence and durability of the Production Guidelines for Book
Longevity of the Council on Library Resources.

❀ This book was produced with environmental mindfulness.
For more information, please visit wisdompubs.org/wisdom-environment.

Printed in the PRC.

Dedicated to Eden, Avrum, and Joshua,
who I hope will always know happiness,
regardless of what they can or cannot do.

Leela loved to do yoga.

She practiced each week
with her best friend Lyle.

They could do all sorts of
fancy poses,

like

downward

dog,

tree pose,

and

cat

pose.

But there was one pose
that Leela couldn't do...

She couldn't do a headstand.

Each time Leela tried,
she counted...

Then she swung her legs
into the air
and...

she shouted from
the floor.

she sighed at

the dinner table.

she mumbled in the washroom.

(Meaning "I can't do it,"
of course.)

And when she tried again before bedtime,

GUESS WHAT HAPPENED?

Leela couldn't do it.
Just like she told herself.

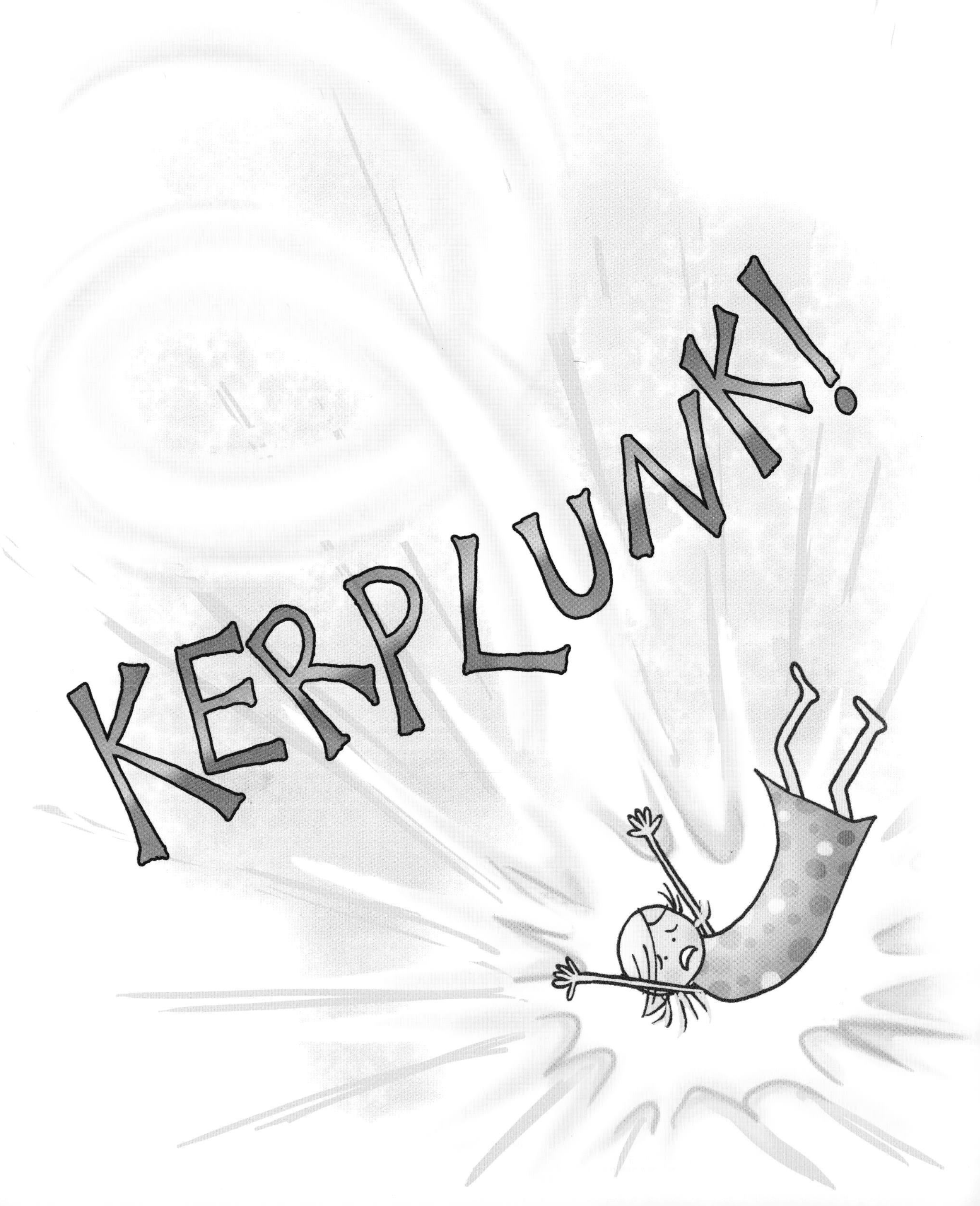
KERPLUNK!

Night after night,
Leela dreamed of all the things
she couldn't do.

One day, Lyle and Leela
went to yoga class.

When some of the children
started doing headstands,

Leela watched them with envy.

Sari sang.

Shauna shouted.

Barry bragged.

"It's too bad YOU can't, too!"

Leela PLOPPED down
on her yoga mat.

"I'M FRUS-TER-A-TED!!!"

she cried.

So Lyle helped Leela.

1...

"I think you've got it!"
Lyle cheered.

2...

"I think I do too!!!"
Leela shouted.
"YOU CAN LET GO NOW!"

3...

After class, as Lyle and Leela
walked home,

Leela tried not to cry.

"If ONLY I could do headstands,"
she said,

"THEN I would be happy."

"But you can do lots of things,"
Lyle said.

"You can ice skate
and sing,
and draw **stars**
in the sand."

"It's TRUE," said Leela, "I can..."

So instead of just waiting
for headstand happiness,

Leela found some fun.

She frolicked in the fall,

she **Whirled** in the winter,

she skipped in the spring,

and as the seasons
changed...

so

did

Leela.

"HA!"

Barry snickered

as he spotted Leela
in the summertime.

"You STILL can't do a headstand?"

"No, not YET!" Leela replied.

"But maybe I'll be able to do one soon.

And even if I can't, there are all sorts of other things I CAN DO!

Just

like

this..."

Then Leela LEAPED
into a somersault

and rolled

down

the hill

laughing.

Because

HAPPINESS

doesn't come
from
headstands.

Message from the Author

Happiness Doesn't Come from Headstands is a tale about patience, friendship, and developing resilience in pursuit of a goal. But at its heart, this book is about a little girl who learns that the journey is more important than the goal itself.

I wrote this story to offer an alternative to *The Little Engine that Could*, which claims that "practice makes perfect." In my experience, no matter how hard we try, there are times we are unable to achieve a goal. And how difficult it is to find peace in those times.

Thankfully, even in the face of failure, peace can be found. By letting go of the idea that happiness depends on achieving a single, external goal, we free ourselves to discover joy from within.

Happiness Doesn't Come from Headstands shares a message I firmly believe: just because we may have a failure, it doesn't mean that we are a failure.

In our achievement-focused world, it's easy to become disheartened by defeat and conclude that happiness is out of reach. It's important to set and obtain goals, but one cannot find self-worth in accomplishment alone. Only in our own perspective can we find true joy.

So invite the children in your life to frolic in the fall and whirl in the winter. Encourage them to celebrate their victories, but also to find compassion for their failures. Accomplishments and challenges are both facets of the wondrous spectrum of life.

My hope is to inspire you as you inspire the children in your life.

Tamara Levitt

Tamara Levitt
Founder of Begin Within Productions
www.beginwithin.ca
@tamaralevitt

Acknowledgment

My deepest thanks to Chris Advansun, whose unwavering belief, steadfast support, and unconditional friendship helped bring this book to life.

Thank you for showing me the meaning of gratitude.